WAKE UP, JEREMIAH

RONALD HIMLER

HARPER & ROW, PUBLISHERS

NEW YORK · HAGERSTOWN · SAN FRANCISCO · LONDON

Wake Up, Jeremiah
Copyright © 1979 by Ronald Himler
All rights reserved. No part of this book may be
used or reproduced in any manner whatsoever without
written permission except in the case of brief quotations
embodied in critical articles and reviews. Printed in
the United States of America. For information address
Harper & Row, Publishers, Inc., 10 East 53rd Street,
New York, N.Y. 10022. Published simultaneously in
Canada by Fitzhenry & Whiteside Limited, Toronto.
First Edition

Library of Congress Cataloging in Publication Data
Himler, Ronald.
Wake up, Jeremiah.

SUMMARY: A small boy runs to a hilltop with the
rising sun and home again to wake his parents.
[1. Sun—Fiction   2. Day—Fiction]   I. Title.
PZ7.H5684Wak   [E]   77-25679
ISBN 0-06-022323-5
ISBN 0-06-022324-3 lib. bdg.

For my son,
PEER

Wake up, Jeremiah! Get out of bed.

It's there at the window.

Dress, Jeremiah! Hurry and dress.

It's on the stairs.

Quick, Jeremiah! Through the house and out the door.

Across the grass and over the wall.

It's in the trees.

Run, Jeremiah, to the top of the hill.

It is there!

Run, Jeremiah. Down the hill

and over the wall.

Across the grass

and onto the porch.

Through the door

and up the stairs.

Wake Mama. Wake Papa. Wake them to the new day.